CW01190886

Eleanor Allitt graduated in textile design at central St Martins. She studied with Cecil Collins and Edward Bawden and worked producing hand block printed silk. Over the last twenty years she has been painting and illustrating and has held sell-out one man shows and had paintings accepted at the Royal Academy and the Royal Watercolour Society. She tells less well known traditional stories in schools and other organisations often accompanied by her own digitally projected illustrations.

Best Wishes Eleanor Allitt 4.11.15

Published in 2010 by print on demand-worldwide.com

Text and illustrations copyright© Eleanor Allitt
The right of Eleanor Allitt to be identified as author and illustrator of this work has been asserted in accordance with the Copyright Designs and Patents Act 1988.

All rights reserved. No part of this book may be reproduced, transmitted or stored in an information retrieval system in any form or by any means, graphic, electronic or mechanical, including photocopying, taping and recording, without prior permission from the author.

www.eleanorallitt.com
www.inannapicturebook.co.uk

I would like to thank many friends for their advice and encouragement while I struggled with the numerous creative and technological mysteries involved with the making of this book. They are in particular Nomi Rowe, Irving Finkel, Heather Algar, Jane and Charles Williams, Andy Minty, and Martin Wells. For photography I would also like to thank Dave Perry.

In addition I would like to thank the British Museum for providing ongoing inspiration.

iv

Sometimes along the river of life we come to a point where a choice presents itself. One way appears attractive, comfortable and safe. The other is less certain, it offers a very different kind of journey, one which beckons us to an unknown country. This way demands great courage, for it is indeed perilous and there is no promise of a safe arrival.

Which of your most precious possessions would you take with you?
Which would you least like to loose?

CASPIAN SEA
MEDITERRANEAN SEA
TIGRIS
EUPRATES
BABYLON
URUK
N
W
E
S
RED SEA
PERSIAN GULF

DARING TO DISCOVER

Inanna, the beautiful young woman from Uruk is happily married to Dumuzi, with two young sons. One day she hears a voice which calls her to visit her sister in the heart of the Underworld. She wants to resist, but the call grows louder until at last she gives in, and prepares for a life-changing journey.

In the first days,
 in the very first days,

In the first nights,
 in the very first nights,

In the first years,
 in the very first years,

All things were set into being.

Heaven and earth became separate from then on.

Water was drawn from the well and bread was baked in the shrines of the land, and each thing was given a name.

There was also an underworld and this was given to Erishkagal.

In those first days there was a young women who in time would become great. She was the daughter of the moon, and the great grand-daughter of the sky god An, and Nannu—mother of heaven and earth.

She was destined to become queen of heaven and earth. Mountains would bow to her, and the skies would reflect her radiance. Her name was Inanna.

She would dare to go down into the darkness of the underworld, and, to find her way back.

Inanna was as beautiful as the morning star that opens the light of day and as serene as the evening star that softly shines to welcome the night.

She loved to dance amongst the green grasses and waving reeds, and to sing in the soft warm air.

She was exuberant, and her delight was in exploring in the meadows amongst the wild flowers. She wanted to give thanks for her great gifts and so she resolved to visit the God Enki.

'I shall go to the deep sweet waters of the sacred river Abzu and say a prayer and honour the great Enki, the God of Wisdom.' she said.

While she was still a little way away Enki whose ears were always wide open and who held great wisdom in his heart, called to his servant and said:

'Inanna is about to enter the holy place, prepare spiced butter cakes for her and fill her glass with cool water. Offer her wine in a sparkIng glass. Greet Inanna with tender love and seat her at the holy table, the table of heaven.'

And so Inanna was welcomed and Enki raised his glass to her and they drank together. Enki was contented, he wanted to make a gift to her, so he stood up and bowed to Inanna, and said:

'In the power of my name, in the power of this holy place, to my daughter Inanna I bestow the perceptive ear, the power of attention, and the art of kindliness.'

And Inanna bowed low and replied: 'I receive them.'

Then Enki raised his glass to Inanna again and said:
'In the power of my name, in the power of this holy place, to my daughter Inanna I bestow the wisdom of discernment, the giving of judgements, and the sifting of the earth to make decisions.'

And again Inanna bowed low and replied:
'I receive them.'

Then Enki raised his glass to Inanna again and said:
'In the power of my name, in the power of this holy place, to my daughter Inanna I give priesthood, and it shall be given with a noble and enduring crown. I shall name you Queen of Heaven and Earth.'

And again Inanna bowed low and replied:
'I receive them.'

Fourteen times Enki raised his glass to Inanna and heaped upon her all the gifts of heaven and earth.

Then Enki raised his glass once again to Inanna and said:
'In the power of my name, in the power of this holy place, to my daughter Inanna I bestow Truth, descent into the underworld, and return from the underworld.'

And Inanna bowed low and replied:
'I receive them.'

And then, a little unsteadily, Enki spoke to his servant and said:
'It is my wish that Inanna returns to her city safely, and with that he fell fast asleep.

Inanna gathered together all the gifts beyond price, and placed them carefully in the Boat of Heaven.

The wind awakened and dancing gently, it carried her safely back to her home city, Uruk.

There was great rejoicing when Inanna entered the city, and joyful celebration took place on the drums, on the timbrel, on the harp and on the flute. Then Inanna brought the Boat of Heaven swiftly to the White Quay in the centre of the city, and the precious gifts were laid in Inanna's holy house. Each one was announced and presented to the people of Sumer.

As the people watched, they delighted to witness all the gifts which radiated from their queen. Their eyes shone with joy to see the gift of womanly grace. Their eyes danced to see the beauty of her rounded breasts. They sang with pleasure to see her charm and poise. They were satisfied with the grace of her sweeping robes and the uprightness of her noble crowned head.

Inanna's great destiny shone over her people They sang to her radiance, and they sang to her beauty and her grace.

Not many months later, while Inanna was out walking in the green hills she noticed a shepherd, he was tall and his dark hair wavy like fresh tide-washed sand, his muscles firm and strong.

His name was Dumuzi.

Does love begin at first sight?

That evening he came down from the hills looking for her, and he found her in the square near her home. She was wearing her blue sky-washed linen shift, and her hair shone like rippling water.

Inanna shone with love. She danced and sang. Over many moons their love increased and in due time their betrothal was announced and Inanna said to her women: 'When Dumuzi comes let the musicians play. I will pour wine for him. I will please his heart. Set sweet herbs and flowers in my room. Put his hand in my hand.

Press his heart next to my heart, our pleasure will be great. I will rest my head on his shoulder and our sleep will be sweet.

Then Dumuzi, the wild bull came into the house treading as lightly as moonlight.

In the fountains there was joy, the fish leapt and danced with delight.
There was a soft light in heaven. Sweet was their love. Two hearts balanced in timeless moments, the stars stopped their movement to honour such a love.

Heaven and earth stood still.

Underground the moles paused and listened. Deer ceased their munching.

On the air the swallows rested, wings outstretched, listening.

In time two sons, Shara and Lulal were born.

Such was their love.

Time passed. And from the Great Above Inanna opened her ear to the Great Below.

The goddess opened her ear to the Great Below.

She set her ear to the Great Below.

14

The underworld called to her, it called in the morning, it called in the evening, and it called at night. Inanna wanted to remain but the call grew louder. The goddess wanted to stay with Dumuzi but the call grew louder. She wanted to be in her sweet paradise with Dumuzi, but the call became insistent.

Inanna's heart was filled with unease, it would be a perilous descent.

She might not return. But .... the sound of the call creeps into her heart and begs her to follow.

Inanna abandons heaven and earth to descend into the underworld.

She gathers together the seven holy gifts, the sacred gifts, and prepares herself.

She places the first gift on her head, the crown of the plane.

She places the second gift of small amethyst beads around her neck.

She puts the third gift, the double strand of small soapstone beads round her breast.

She puts the fourth gift, the shining gold ring on her finger.

She binds the fifth gift, the breastplate of engraved gold close to her breast.

She takes the sixth gift, the lapis measuring rod and line in her hand.
She slips the seventh gift, the royal robe of velvet round her body.

Inanna sets out for the Underworld.
She abandons her temples to descend to the underworld.
She bids her beloved Dumuzi farewell.

Her faithful friend Ninshubur accompanies her.
Inanna prepares her lest she should not return, lest she should die. So she lays her hand on her shoulders and says:

'Ninshubar, my faithful servant, my warrior who fights by my side, my most valued friend, hear me. If after three days I have not returned set up a lament for me. Put ashes on your face in mourning, dress in sackcloth, then visit the god Enki for me. Ask him to save me.
With your whole body stretch out and implore him to help me.'

Do not let your daughter be put to death in the underworld,

Do not let the bright silver of her statue become covered in the dust of yesterday.

Do not let the precious lapis be shattered into random pieces.

Do not let the fragrant boxwood be broken and destroyed.

Do not let the holy priestess be put to death in the underworld.

Enki has been to the underworld and returned.

He alone is the one who knows the food of life. He alone is the one who knows the water of life. He knows the secrets, the holy secrets.

Surely he will not let me die.'

When Inanna arrived at the outer gate of the Underworld she knocked loudly and cried out in a strong voice:

'Open the door, gatekeeper, open the door for Inanna, I am alone and travelling to the east, and I have to pass through this gate.'

Neti the gatekeeper fixed her face with his stone-cold eye and said:

'Why do you travel this way, why has your heart fastened on this road, a road from which no traveller returns?'
Inanna replied:

'Because of my older sister Eriskkagal. Her husband has died and I have come to support her at the funeral rites. Go, tell her that Inanna waits to be allowed to enter her land of motionless darkness.'

So Neti the gatekeeper of the underworld went to Erishkagal and delivered the message.

'A queen Inanna, as tall as heaven, as strong as the earth and as constant as the foundations of the city walls waits outside the palace gates.

She comes prepared with the seven holy protective gifts.'

When the dark queen Erishkagal heard this she bit her lip and flashed her glittering eyes and without delay said these things:

'Listen closely Neti. Bolt the seven gates of the underworld. If my sister, who calls herself Queen of heaven and earth, truly wishes to enter my kingdom, then at each gate she must give up one of the seven gifts. She will enter my kingdom bowed low. She will enter my kingdom with nothing. She will enter my kingdom naked.'

Neti heeded his queen's words and he bolted the seven gates of the Underworld. Then he opened the outer gate and said:

'Come Inanna, give me your crown and you may enter.'

From her head the radiant crown was removed. Inanna, struggling, gasped

'What is happening?' Neti turned, and with stonehard voice he said:
'Quiet Inanna, do not complain about the decrees of this place.
The laws of the Underworld may not be questioned.'

The steps led down down down, into the Underworld. The way was narrow, the way was dark.
Inanna inched her way down, fearing at each step that she might slip and fall and be lost in hopeless night.
After a hundred steps she found the second gate.
She shook the chain in the velvet hard darkness.

She startled to feel the gatekeepers cold hands as he removed the amethyst beads from round her neck. Inanna whispered 'What is happening?' The gatekeeper turned, and with stone-hard voice he said:

'Quiet Inanna, do not complain about the decrees of this place. The laws of the underworld may not be questioned.'

The steps led down, down, down, into the Underworld. The way was narrow, the way was dark. Inanna inched her way down, fearing at each step that she might fall and be lost in hopeless night.

After a hundred steps she found the third gate. It was carved from stone, massive, cold. She shuddered when the gatekeeper, with ice-cold fingers, touched the back of her neck as he removed the double string of soapstone beads.

'What is happening?' she stuttered. The gatekeeper turned, and with stone-hard voice he said:

'Quiet Inanna, do not complain about the decrees of this place. The laws of the underworld may not be questioned.'

The steps led down, down, down, into the Underworld. The way was narrow, the way was dark. Inanna inched her way down, fearing at each step that she might fall and be lost in hopeless night.

Down another hundred dark damp steps and she came to the fourth gate. This one was made entirely from writhing snakes who silently hissed in the gloom, their eyes gleaming, , their tongues flickering.

A quiet voice whispered into her ear and said:

'Abandon hope all ye who enter here.'

Her gold ring was slowly slid from her finger, removed by unseen hands

'What is happening?' Inanna cried. The gatekeeper turned, and with stone-hard voice he replied:
'Quiet Inanna, do not complain about the decrees of this place. The laws of the underworld may not be questioned.'

The steps led down, down, down, into the underworld, the way was narrow, the way was dark. Inanna inched her way down, fearing at each step that she might fall and be lost in hopeless night.

A further one hundred steps and the fifth gate stood half buried in water. Inanna waded waist-deep in the icy cold and, as she passed through the iron door, invisible hands removed her engraved gold breastplate.

At the sixth gate there was such a weeping and wailing, an anguish beyond comprehension. Inanna, fainting with fear, knocked at the mighty door. From out of her hand the lapis rod and line were taken.
What is happening?' Inanna cried. The gatekeeper turned and with stone-hard voice he replied:

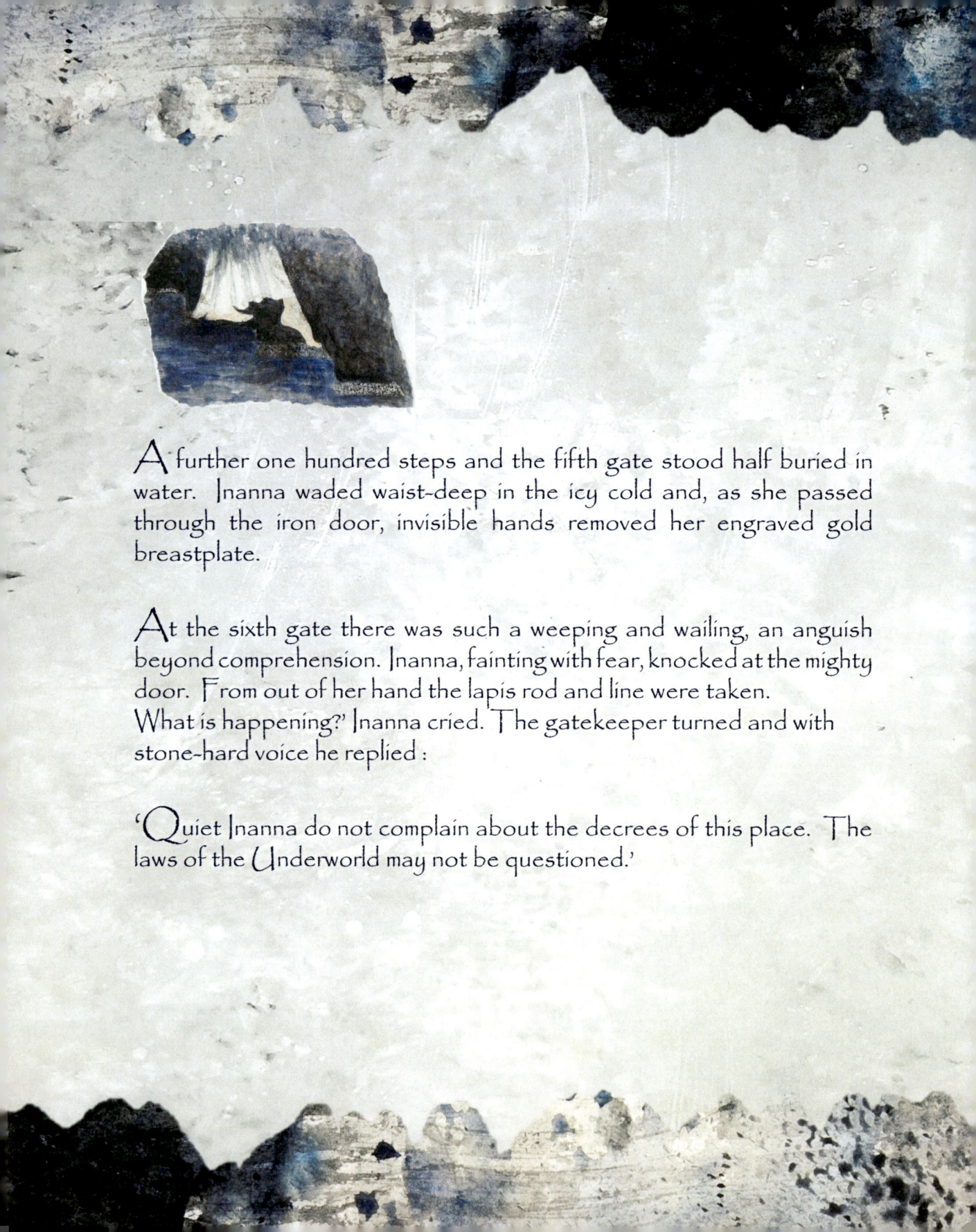

'Quiet Inanna do not complain about the decrees of this place. The laws of the Underworld may not be questioned.'

The steps led down, down, down, into the Underworld. The way was narrow, the way was dark. Inanna inched her way down, fearing at each step that she might fall and be lost in hopeless night.

The seventh gate was carved from Ice. Motionless it stood, eerie light glowing from its massive columns.

Silently the royal robe was removed from her body.

'What is happening?' Inanna whispered. The gatekeeper turned, and with stone-hard voice he said:

'Quiet Inanna, do not complain about the decrees of this place. The laws of the Underworld may not be questioned.'

Now she stood at the very heart of the underworld.

Naked and bowed low Inanna entered the throne room.

Erishkigal rose from her throne and signalled to the Anunni, the seven judges of the underworld.

The heartless ones immediately approached and surrounded her. With one voice they passed judgement on her.

Then Erishkagal fastened upon Inanna the eye of death.

She spoke against her the word of wrath.

She uttered against her the sentence of guilt.

She struck her down.

31

Inanna's
Naked
body
was
Hung
from
A
Hook
On
The wall.

Ninshubur waited patiently for her friend and mistress.

She waited three days and three nights. And then, when Inanna still had not returned she set up a lament, dressed herself in sackcloth, and put ashes on her face set out alone for the temple of Father Enki.

When she entered the shrine she cried out:

'O Father Enki, do not let your daughter be put to death in the Underworld.'

He sat quietly, eyes downcast, listening with his third eye.

Then, quietly he said:

'What has happened? What has my daughter done? I fear for her, my daughter, my precious daughter.'

And he sighed a long, deep sigh.

Then from under the finger nails of his right hand he found some earth, and he modelled it in his hands, and made a little tiny creature, neither male nor female. To this creature he gave the most precious gift, the food of life. Then he found some earth under the fingernails of his left hand and with this he made another little tiny creature, to this one he gave the most precious gift, the water of life.

Then he said to the little creatures 'Take these gifts to the Underworld. You can fly through the seven gates with ease, and like flies you can make your way past the guards and enter Erishkagal's chamber. There you will find her in travail. She is as a women about to give birth. You will find her with no linen spread over her. Her breasts are uncovered and her hair swirls about like a garden of wild leeks. She writhes upon the floor in agony.

When she groans Oh my stomach, moan with her, when she groans Oh my joints and skin, moan with her. This will please her and she will offer you a gift. Do not accept anything but the body of Inanna, the corpse that hangs from the hook on the wall. Then sprinkle over it the precious gifts, the food of life and the water of life.'

Enki's tiny creatures set out for the Underworld, and like flies they flew down, down, down the narrow steps.

They flew through the seven gates so quietly that no gatekeeper noticed them. They silently entered Erishkagal's throne room.

There they found her.

She cried out in great travail. As she moaned, so the flies moaned with her. They gave her the gift of compassion.

All at once the moaning stopped, the Queen of the Underworld felt better. She looked up and saw the flies and said:

'I bless you, I too want to give you a gift. I will give you the water gift, the river in it's fullness.'

'We cannot accept it,' replied the flies.

'I will give you the grain gift, the fields in harvest.'

'We cannot accept it,' replied the flies.

'We wish only for the corpse that hangs from the hook on the wall.'

The corpse was unhooked and given to them. It was laid on the floor before them. They sprinkled it with the food of life, and with the water of life.

Inanna's eyes opened,

and life came back to her.

Inanna stood up and made to leave the underworld, but the seven fearsome judges, the Anunni, who have never tasted food or drink, who never accept gifts, and who have never felt a lover's embrace or a child's kiss, took hold of her with their bone-hard hands.

Inanna tried to step
forward but the crowd of
demons enclosed her
'No-one ascends
from the Underworld
unmarked.

If you wish to return you
must find someone to take
your place.'

Then they showed her Ninshubar waiting patiently in the Great Above and they said:

'Watch carefully Inanna, we will take Ninshubar in your place.'

But Inanna cried:

'No! Ninshubar is my companion, my constant support. She gives me wise council, she is a warrior by my side. She did not forget my words, she mourned for me. Because of her my life was saved. I will never give Ninshubar to you.'

Then the Anunni showed Inanna her son Shara, dressed in sackcloth.

'Watch carefully Inanna, Shara can come in your place.'

But Inanna cried:

'No you cannot take Shara he is my son, you cannot take him.'

Then the Anunni showed the Inanna her son Lulal, but again Inanna cried:

'No, you cannot take Lulal, he is my son.'

Then the Anunni said to Inanna:
'Watch carefully, we will show you Dumuzi. We will allow you to be present in the great Above and to talk to him.'

Dimly at first and then quite clearly, Inanna could see him. He sat on a magnificent throne, dressed in splendid robes and with a crown on his head and a sceptre in his hand.

'You have done nothing to help me, you have not thought about me. You have done nothing to help me.' She judged Dumuzi and found him guilty. And she said to the Anunni:

'Take him,' and they went to seize him.

46

Then Dumuzi raised his hands to heaven to Utu the God of Justice and beseeched him:

'Utu, you are a just God, a merciful God, change my hands into the heads of snakes, and my feet into the tails of snakes, let me escape from the Anunni, do not let them carry me away.'

The merciful Utu accepted Dumuzi's tears and granted his request and Dumuzi escaped from the demons with his snakehead hands and his snaketail feet and hid under a rock.

He fell into a deep sleep and had a strange dream. When he awoke his heart was full of tears and he called out for his sister Geshtinanna.

'Bring my sister, my little sister, my scribe, my singer who knows more than all my songs. My wise woman who knows the meaning of dreams, I must speak to her.'

When she appeared he started to recount his dream, how the tall rushes had grown so close to him and how the double reed had trembled.

And how the eagle had seized a lamb in the sheepfold and how the falcon had snatched a sparrow in the reed fence.

Geshtinanna put her head on his shoulder and replied :

'Even the snakehead hands and snaketail feet cannot save you. My hair swirls around in heaven for you, and my sheep scratch the earth with bent feet, Oh Dumuzi I grieve for you.

There is no escape for you.'

And even as she said these words a mighty wind engulfed Dumuzi and he was bound up and carried away.

When Inanna saw this she wept bitterly for her beloved husband. 'Dumuzi has been taken away, he will no longer raise his sword in battle, he will no longer soap himself in the holy shrine. My wild bull has been taken away before I could wrap him in a burial shroud.

You ask me about his reed flute? The wind must play it for him.

You ask me about his sweet songs? The wind must sing them for him.

My heart plays the reed pipe in mourning. Once Dumuzi wandered so freely over the plains now he is bound.

There is grief in the inmost chambers of my heart.'

Geshtinanna, Dumuzi's sister also wandered about in desolation weeping for her brother.

'Oh Dumuzi I weep for you. I want to find my brother, I want to comfort him. I want to share his fate.'

When Inanna saw the grief of Geshtinanna she said:
'I want to take you to him but I do not know where they have laid him.'

Then a fly appeared. The tiny fly buzzed around Inanna's head and landed on her ear. Then it spoke into her ear:

'If I tell you where Dumuzi is, what will you give me?' Inanna replied:

'I will give you knowledge of all gossip. You will hear life in the beer-house, in the taverns, in the houses. You will crouch on the walls, the ceilings and the corners of the windows. You will hear everything men say.'

Then the fly replied:

'I will tell you where they have laid him. Lift your eyes to the edges of the plane, there you will find the shepherd Dumuzi.'

Inanna and Geshtinanna hastened to the edge of the plane and there they found Dumuzi, weeping. Inanna took his hand in hers and said:

'Because we are one, because we are like two halves of an apple, you will go to the underworld for only half the year.

Your sister, has given you her Greatest gift. She will go for the other half of the year. On the day you are called, on that day you will be taken.

On the day Geshtinanna is called, on that day she, will be taken and you will return.

Our love will lie dormant for half the year, but on your return it will arise and be rekindled.'

When Erishkagal heard this she was satisfied.

She recalled Inanna, and then ordered the great gate of the innermost region of the Underworld to be opened.

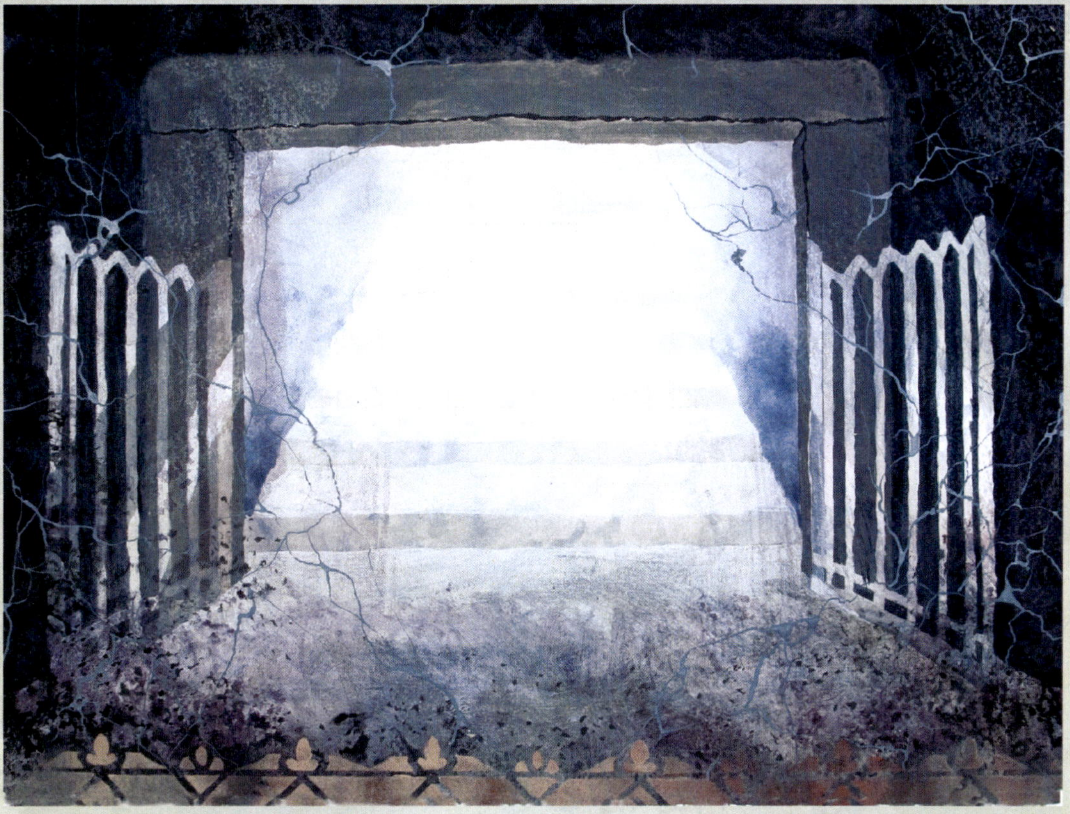

As Inanna passed through it the gatekeeper gave her back her royal robe.

At the sixth gate, the gatekeeper gave her back her lapis rod and line.

At the fifth gate the gatekeeper gave her back her engraved gold breastplate.

At the fourth gate the gatekeeper gave her back her shining gold ring.

At the third gate the gatekeeper gave her back her double string of soapstone beads.

At the second gate the gatekeeper gave her back her small necklace of amethyst beads.

At the first gate the gatekeeper gave her back her radiant crown.

Now Inanna,

Queen of Heaven and Earth

had returned to the Great Above.

The sun shone on her as she walked forward.